Opening Day

Susan Bartlett

Illustrated by Luanne Wrenn

TILBURY HOUSE PUBLISHERS

GARDINER, MAINE

"Four-thirty!"

Sam woke up as soon as he heard his father call. He pushed off the warm covers and swung his bare feet onto the cold floor. He was both excited and worried.

It was the opening day of deer season and he was going hunting for the first time. Shivering, he pulled on his long underwear, woolen pants, shirt, and socks, and then laced up his leather boots.

"I'm wearing enough clothes for the whole sixth grade," Sam complained to his mother in the kitchen.

"Now do exactly what Mr. Cundy tells you," said Sam's father. "No goofing around with Eric."

Eric Cundy, Sam's best friend, had been hunting since he was eight. "Our family's always hunted," Eric had told Sam. "Mom, too."

"Really?" Sam had been impressed. No one in his family hunted. His parents did not believe in killing animals.

"Maybe if we had nothing else to eat," his father said. "But the supermarket's down the road, and I say let the animals live."

But Sam wanted to make up his own mind. His parents had finally agreed. He had taken a hunter education course and earned the certificate that meant he could apply for a hunting license. All fall he and Eric had talked about the fun they would have in the woods with Eric's dad. Eric's sister, who was hunting today with her grandmother, had loaned Sam one of her guns. After some practice, he turned out to be a good shot.

The lights on Mr. Cundy's pickup flashed in the driveway. Sam slipped his pack over one shoulder. In the pack were snacks, water, a compass, first-aid kit, and waterproof matches.

His father looped a whistle around Sam's neck. "To signal in case you get lost."

"Dad, please." Sam groaned. "I'm not getting lost." Outside the wind stung his cheeks and his breath made tiny frosty clouds in the icy air. It was still dark as night.

Inside the truck he and Eric swapped high fives.

"All set?" Eric asked.

"I'm cool," Sam said, not wanting to admit he was nervous.

"I'll treat you both to breakfast," said Mr. Cundy.

The Moosehead Diner was full of hunters. Sam's neighbors were there plus Mr. Shaw, the minister, and some teachers from school. Sam and Eric ordered pancakes, maple syrup, and their first cup of coffee ever.

"Initiation," said Mr. Cundy, smiling.

"Not bad," said Sam after he took a swallow.

"Tastes like dog poop," said Eric.

"How do you know?" Sam grinned.

When they left the diner, friends waved and wished them good hunting.
It made Sam feel great.

They parked the pickup at the edge of a big field near Boulder Rock.
It was lighter now, the sky whitening in the east. A fine snow was falling.

"Are those deer tracks?" Sam asked. The hoof marks looked like little bananas
with dots behind them. He slipped his gun from his shoulder so fast he almost
dropped it. "I'm loading."

"Not yet," said Mr. Cundy. "Remember, we don't hike in with loaded guns."

Sam felt like a dope. Of course, he knew that. He wondered what he would do
when a deer actually came. Maybe he'd panic and do something even more stupid.

"I promised Mom we'd fill the freezer," said Eric.

"We all like deer meat," Mr. Cundy said. "And Eric's mom usually treats the
neighbors to her venison stew." That was another thing Sam liked about the
Cundys. He knew they didn't have a lot of money, but they were generous.

Sam thought of his own freezer, filled with vegetables from the summer garden.
If he got a deer today, he'd give it to the Cundys. He knew his parents wouldn't
eat it. Mom was a total vegetarian—Dad, almost.

They crossed a wide meadow and started down a logging road overgrown with wild raspberries and frost-blackened fern. Thorns caught in their bootlaces and on their socks. The road climbed into a stand of white pine and then snaked low into a tangle of windfalls. Sam touched the front of his vest to make sure his hunting license was still clipped tight.

"We're headed for a place we scouted last week," said Mr. Cundy.

"I found it first," bragged Eric. "It's got lots of deer sign. Scrapes and rubs." Sometimes Eric seemed to know everything, Sam thought. He looked up as a bird spiraled out of a hemlock.

"Hey!" he called, proud of himself. "A red-tailed hawk." At least he knew birds.

"Let's be quiet," said Mr. Cundy. "If you even step on a branch, you'll spook the deer." Suddenly he froze. Sam and Eric stopped short.

A deer!

Browsing on a cedar. Sam was so surprised
he stepped back and came down hard on a stick.
It cracked!
The deer flicked its tail and looked up. Sam stopped breathing.
After a while, it started eating again. It was a doe. They couldn't shoot a doe, even if
the guns had been loaded. Their hunting permits were only for bucks.

"Awesome," whispered Sam. "I've never been this close to a deer before."

"Deer can hear much better than people," Mr. Cundy said after they had backed away.
"Their ears catch sound and amplify it."

"They're also super smellers," said Eric. "Ten thousand times better than us." Sam knew
that was why hunters walked into the wind—so it would blow their scent away from
any deer up ahead. They hiked another half mile.

"Here it is!" said Eric, pleased with himself. He pointed to the ground under some hemlocks.

"What are those?" Sam stared at some big swishes in the leaves and dirt.

"The bucks make those to attract does," said Mr. Cundy. "Then they rub the tree over the scrape and squeeze scent from their eyes onto the trunk."

"Weird, huh?" Eric sniffed the tree. "They rub their back legs, too, to make more scent. Then they pee and it runs into the scrape."

"Yuk!" said Sam. "It must stink."

"It does," said Eric, "but the does like it."

"If we wait here long enough, we should see something." Mr. Cundy eased off his pack and gun and sat down with his back against a tree.

"I'm pigging out." Eric bit into a blueberry muffin.

Sam tore the wrapping off a granola bar and wondered how long they would stay.
Hunting sure took patience.

"We can load now,"
said Mr. Cundy.
"Make sure your
safety's on."

Sam and Eric each
loaded three rounds.
As Sam touched the
ammo, he felt uneasy.
This is real, he thought,
as he worked the bolt to
chamber the first round.
And he imagined the doe again.
She looked so strong and pretty.
Did he really want to shoot a deer?

Still, think how impressed the guys
would be at school if he got a buck on
the first day out.

Suddenly, rat, tat, tat! Real loud! Everyone started.

Sam smiled. He knew bird calls. A pileated woodpecker
was thwacking for ants. It had a bill like a hammer.

Something rustled in the leaves. "It's got to be a deer," Eric said softly.
Wrong. It was a squirrel. Three squirrels.
They jabbered and made an awful racket.

Maybe no deer will come, Sam thought now. Maybe I'll be glad.
Maybe I don't want to shoot. Can deer hear heartbeats?
Mine are really loud.

Eric stood up to stretch. "I'm freezing," he mouthed.

Mr. Cundy signaled. Something's coming!

Sam stared.

Nothing.

Then in the trees he saw the top of an antler. Just barely.

The antlers moved. He saw a head.

The deer stepped out into the open.

Holy cow! thought Sam. It's huge.

It was a buck with a big rack. A twelve-pointer at least.
Eric slipped off his safety. So did Mr. Cundy.

Sam's hands were shaking. He tried to steady his elbows
on his knees and fix the deer in the crosshairs of his scope.
But it was bouncing around like crazy.

Should he shoot? He hesitated and turned to look at Eric.

The deer saw Sam move.
His tail flagged and he snorted.
He leaped and turned.

Mr. Cundy fired.   So did Eric.

The bullets tore through the branches and disappeared.

"He's gone." Mr. Cundy shook his head. They walked forward to make sure no one had wounded the deer. They found no blood or hair on the trail. It was a clean miss.

"We should have gotten it." Eric kicked hard at the snow and it flew from his boots onto Sam's jacket. "We were so close." He scowled.

"Sorry," Sam mumbled, thinking it was his fault. He looked down at his gun, embarrassed, and then he felt guilty because he was relieved that the deer got away.

"That's okay," said Mr. Cundy. "It happens.
Any hunter can move at the wrong moment.
Next time we won't miss."

They ate lunch and then staked out an apple orchard. A buck and a doe walked into
the apple trees, but Mr. Cundy sneezed and the deer kicked up and ran. The sneeze
made Sam feel better about his own mistake.

It was getting colder. The wind blew snow from overhead branches.
The flakes settled on Sam's jacket and slipped down his collar.

"Time to head home," said Mr. Cundy. "It'll be dark soon and I'm hungry
as a bear in spring."

"One more stakeout, please?" begged Eric.

Sam's toes felt like Popsicles, and he kept thinking of pizza instead of deer sign.
He crossed fingers that Mr. Cundy would say no.

"Nope. We want to be alive and breathing when we get back," Mr. Cundy joked.
"Sam can lead. I've noticed he's a fine hiker."

"Thanks." Sam thought how nice Mr. Cundy was, and picked up the trail.
They started back to the pickup.

"Want to come tomorrow?" Eric asked as they reached the field near
Boulder Rock. "We've scouted another place. Bracketts' pasture."

"Thanks." Sam hesitated. "I'm glad I came, but—"

"But what? You can't quit. The season's just started." Eric poked at Sam's hunting license and Sam thought of how proud he had been when he bought it.

He didn't want to let Eric down. It would be easy to say yes and try again. But he was pretty sure he wasn't going to be a hunter. It was okay for lots of people. But not for him. At least not now.

"Can't we just target practice together?" Sam asked.

"Come on, Sam. You can't quit," said Eric.

"I bet I get more bull's-eyes than you." Sam wanted Eric to say something to show he wasn't mad.

"No way, goofball." Eric took the dare. He punched Sam's arm. "You're on."

"I'll set up a target for you," said Mr. Cundy.

"Deal," said Sam, happy now. Ahead he saw the truck, dusted with snow.

"Want to come for supper?" he asked Eric.

"Sure," said Eric. "As long as you're not having tofu."

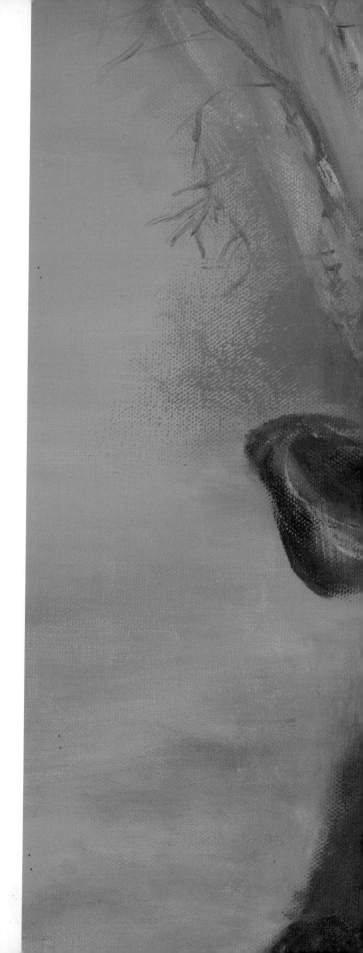

TILBURY HOUSE, PUBLISHERS

2 Mechanic Street, Gardiner, Maine 04345   800-582-1899 • www.tilburyhouse.com

First hardcover printing: May 2007 • 10 9 8 7 6 5 4 3 2 1

For Seward, who cherished the natural world. —SB

Dedicated to my wonderful family and friends who modeled for the characters in this book. —LW

The author acknowledges with gratitude the suggestions of Lou Haskell, Maine Department of Inland Fisheries and Wildlife; Eric Nuse, former hunter education coordinator, Vermont Fish and Wildlife; Chris Saunders, Vermont Fish and Wildlife; Mark Gocke, Wyoming Game and Fish; and Dave Wilson, Ohio Division of Wildlife.

Library of Congress Cataloging-in-Publication Data

Weber, Susan Bartlett.

Opening day / Susan Bartlett ; illustrated by Luanne Wrenn.

    p. cm.

Summary: Having taken a hunter education course and gotten a license, Sam feels ready for his first hunting trip with his best friend Eric and Eric's father, but once he gets close to a deer he is not certain he wants to shoot one.

ISBN-13: 978-0-88448-288-8 (hardcover : alk. paper)

[1. Hunting—Fiction. 2. Deer—Fiction. 3. Conduct of life—Fiction.] I. Wrenn, Luanne, 1961- ill. II. Title.

PZ7.W3896Ope 2007

[Fic]—dc22

2006037839

Designed by Geraldine Millham, Westport, Massachusetts

Printed by Sung In Printing, South Korea